GOOD LADY DUCAYNE

BY

MARY ELIZABETH BRADDON

British Library Cataloguing-in-Publication Data
A catalogue record for this book is available from the
British Library

Contents

Miss Braddon

Mary Elizabeth Braddon was born in Soho, London, England in 1835. She was educated privately in England and France, and at the age of just nineteen was offered a commission by a local printer to produce a serial novel "combining the humour of Dickens with the plot and construction of G. P. R. Reynolds" What emerged was *Three Times dead, or The Secret of the Heath,* which was published five years later under the title *The Trail of the Serpent* (1861).

For the rest of her life, Braddon was an extremely prolific writer, producing more than eighty novels, while also finding time to write and act in a number of stage plays. Her most famous novel, *Lady Audley's Secret,* began serialisation in 1862, and was an overnight success, propelling her into fame and fortune. A quintessential 'sensation novel', centring on an incident of "accidental bigamy," *Lady Audley's Secret* has never been out of print, and was adapted as recently as 2000. Braddon also founded *Belgravia Magazine,* and edited *Temple Bar Magazine.* She died in 1915 in Richmond, England, aged 79.

GOOD LADY DUCAYNE

CHAPTER I

Bella Rolleston had made up her mind that her only chance of earning her bread and helping her mother to an occasional crust was by going out into the great unknown world as companion to a lady. She was willing to go to any lady rich enough to pay her a salary and so eccentric as to wish for a hired companion. Five shillings told off reluctantly from one of those sovereigns which were so rare with the mother and daughter, and which melted away so quickly, five solid shillings, had been handed to a smartly-dressed lady in an office in Harbeck Street, W., in the hope that this very Superior Person would find a situation and a salary for Miss Rolleston.

The Superior Person glanced at the two half-crowns as they lay on the table where Bella's hand had placed them, to make sure they were neither of them forms, before she wrote a description of Bella's qualifications and requirements in a formidable-looking ledger.

'Age?' she asked curtly.

'Eighteen, last July.'

'Any accomplishments?'

'No; I am not at all accomplished. If I were I should want to be a governess--a companion seems the lowest stage.'

'We have some highly accomplished ladies on our books as companions, or chaperon companions.'

'Oh, I know!' babbled Bella, loquacious in her youthful candour. 'But that is quite a different thing. Mother hasn't been able to afford a piano since I was twelve years old, so I'm afraid I've forgotten how to play. And I have had to help mother with her needlework, so there hasn't been much time to study.'

'Please don't waste time upon explaining what you can't do, but kindly tell me anything you can do,' said the Superior Person, crushingly, with her pen poised between delicate fingers waiting to write. 'Can you read aloud for two or three hours at a stretch? Are you active and handy, an early riser, a good walker, sweet tempered, and obliging?'

'I can say yes to all those questions except about the sweetness. I think I have a pretty good temper, and I should be anxious to oblige anybody who paid for my services. I should want them to feel that I was really earning my salary.'

'The kind of ladies who come to me would not care for a talkative companion,' said the Person, severely, having finished writing in her book. 'My connection lies chiefly

4

among the aristocracy, and in that class considerable deference is expected.'

'Oh, of course,' said Bella; 'but it's quite different when I'm talking to you. I want to tell you all about myself once and for ever.'

'I am glad it is to be only once!' said the Person, with the edges of her lips.

The Person was of uncertain age, tightly laced in a black silk gown. She had a powdery complexion and a handsome clump of somebody else's hair on the top of her head. It may be that Bella's girlish freshness and vivacity had an irritating effect upon nerves weakened by an eight hours day in that over-heated second floor in Harbeck Street. To Bella the official apartment, with its Brussels carpet, velvet curtains and velvet chairs, and French clock, ticking loud on the marble chimney-piece, suggested the luxury of a palace, as compared with another second floor in Walworth where Mrs Rolleston and her daughter had managed to exist for the last six years.

'Do you think you have anything on your books that would suit me?' faltered Bella, after a pause.

'Oh, dear, no; I have nothing in view at present,' answered the Person, who had swept Bella's half-crowns into a drawer, absentmindedly, with the tips of her fingers. 'You see, you are so very unformed--so much too young to be companion to a lady of position. It is a pity you have not enough education for a nursery governess; that would be more in your line.'

'And do you think it will be very long before you can get me a situation?' asked Bella, doubtfully.

'I really cannot say. Have you any particular reason for being so impatient--not a love affair, I hope?'

'A love affair!' cried Bella, with flaming cheeks. 'What utter nonsense. I want a situation because mother is poor, and I hate being a burden to her. I want a salary that I can share with her.'

'There won't be much margin for sharing in the salary you are likely to get at your age--and with your--very-- unformed manners,' said the Person, who found Bella's peony cheeks, bright eyes, and unbridled vivacity more and more oppressive.

'Perhaps if you'd be kind enough to give me back the fee I could take it to an agency where the connection isn't quite so aristocratic,' said Bella, who--as she told her mother in her recital of the interview--was determined not to be sat upon.

'You will find no agency that can do more for you than mine,' replied the Person, whose harpy fingers never relinquished coin. 'You will have to wait for your opportunity. Yours is an exceptional case: but I will bear you in mind, and if anything suitable offers I will write to you. I cannot say more than that.'

The half-contemptuous bend of the stately head, weighted with borrowed hair, indicated the end of the interview. Bella went back to Walworth--tramped sturdily every inch of the way in the September afternoon--and 'took off' the Superior Person for the amusement of her mother and the landlady, who lingered in the shabby litle sitting--room after bringing in the tea-tray, to applaud Miss Rolleston's 'taking off'.

'Dear, dear, what a mimic she is!' said the landlady. 'You ought to have let her go on the stage, mum. She might have made her fortune as a hactress.'

CHAPTER II

Bella waited and hoped, and listened for the postman's knocks which brought such store of letters for the parlours and the first floor, and so few for that humble second floor, where mother and daughter sat sewing with hand and with wheel and treadle, for the greater part of the day.

Mrs Rolleston was a lady by birth and education; but it had been her bad fortune to marry a scoundrel; for the last half--dozen years she had been that worst of widows, a wife whose husband had deserted her. Happily, she was courageous, industrious, and a clever needle-woman; and she had been able just to earn a living for herself and her only child, by making mantles and cloaks for a West-end house. It was not a luxurious living. Cheap lodgings in a shabby street off the Walworth Road, scanty dinners, homely food, well-worn raiment, had been the portion of mother and daughter; but they loved each other so dearly, and Nature had made them both so light-hearted, that they had contrived somehow to be happy..But now this idea of going out into the world as companion to some fine lady had rooted itself into Bella's mind, and although she idolized her mother, and although the parting of mother and daughter must needs tear two loving hearts into shreds, the girl longed for enterprise and change and excitement, as the pages of old

longed to be knights, and to start for the Holy Land to break
a lance with the infidel.

She grew tired of racing downstairs every time the
postman knocked, only to be told 'nothing for you, miss,'
by the smudgy-faced drudge who picked up the letters from
the passage floor.

'Nothing for you, miss,' grinned the lodging-house
drudge, till at last Bella took heart of grace and walked up
to Harbeck Street, and asked the Superior Person how it was
that no situation had been found for her.

'You are too young,' said the Person, 'and you want a
salary.'

'Of course I do,' answered Bella; 'don't other people
want salaries?'

'Young ladies of your age generally want a comfortable
home.

'I don't,' snapped Bella; 'I want to help mother.'

'You can call again this day week,' said the Person; 'or, if
I hear of anything in the meantime, I will write to you.

No letter came from the Person, and in exactly a week
Bella put on her neatest hat, the one that had been seldomest
caught in the rain, and trudged off to Harbeck Street.

It was a dull October afternoon, and there was a
greyness in the air which might turn to fog before night. The
Walworth Road shops gleamed brightly through that grey
atmosphere, and though to a young lady reared in Mayfair

or Belgravia such shop-windows would have been unworthy of a glance, they were a snare and temptation for Bella. There were so many things that she longed for, and would never be able to buy.

Harbeck Street is apt to be empty at this dead season of the year, a long, long street, an endless perspective of eminently respectable houses. The Person's office was at the further end, and Bella looked down that long, grey vista almost despairingly, more tired than usual with the trudge from Walworth. As she looked, a carriage passed her, an old-fashioned, yellow chariot, on cee springs, drawn by a pair of high grey horses, with the stateliest of coachmen driving them, and a tall footman sitting by his side.

'It looks like the fairy god-mother's coach,' thought Bella. 'I shouldn't wonder if it began by being a pumpkin.'

It was a surprise when she reached the Person's door to find the yellow chariot standing before it, and the tall footman waiting near the doorstep. She was almost afraid to go in and meet the owner of that splendid carriage. She had caught only a glimpse of its occupant as the chariot rolled by, a plumed bonnet, a patch of ermine.

The Person's smart page ushered her upstairs and knocked at the official door. 'Miss Rolleston,' he announced, apologetically, while Bella waited outside.

'Show her in,' said the Person, quickly; and then Bella heard her murmuring something in a low voice to her client.

Bella went in fresh, blooming, a living image of youth and hope, and before she looked at the Person her gaze was riveted by the owner of the chariot.

Never had she seen anyone as old as the old lady sitting by the Person's fire: a little old figure, wrapped from chin to feet in an ermine mantle; a withered, old face under a plumed bonnet--a face so wasted by age that it seemed only a pair of eyes and a peaked chin. The nose was peaked, too, but between the sharply pointed chin and the great, shining eyes, the small, aquiline nose was hardly visible..'This is Miss Rolleston, Lady Ducayne.'

Claw-like fingers, flashing with jewels, lifted a double eyeglass to Lady Ducayne's shining black eyes, and through the glasses Bella saw those unnaturally bright eyes magnified to a gigantic size, and glaring at her awfully.

'Miss Torpinter has told me all about you,' said the old voice that belonged to the eyes. 'Have you good health? Are you strong and active, able to eat well, sleep well, walk well, able to enjoy all that there is good in life?'

'I have never known what it is to be ill, or idle,' answered Bella.

'Then I think you will do for me.'

'Of course, in the event of references being perfectly satisfactory,' put in the Person.

'I don't want references. The young woman looks frank and innocent. I'll take her on trust.'

'So like you, dear Lady Ducayne,' murmured Miss Torpinter.

'I want a strong young woman whose health will give me no trouble.'

'You have been so unfortunate in that respect,' cooed the Person, whose voice and manner were subdued to a melting sweetness by the old woman's presence.

'Yes, I've been rather unlucky,' grunted Lady Ducayne.

'But I am sure Miss Rolleston will not disappoint you, though certainly after your unpleasant experience with Miss Tomson, who looked the picture of health--and Miss Blandy, who said she had never seen a doctor since she was vaccinated--'

'Lies, no doubt,' muttered Lady Ducayne, and then turning to Bella, she asked, curtly, 'You don't mind spending the winter in Italy, I suppose?'

In Italy! The very word was magical. Bella's fair young face flushed crimson.

'It has been the dream of my life to see Italy,' she gasped.

From Walworth to Italy! How far, how impossible such a journey had seemed to that romantic dreamer.

'Well, your dream will be realized. Get yourself ready to leave Charing Cross by the train deluxe this day week at eleven. Be sure you are at the station a quarter before the hour. My people will look after you and your luggage.'

Lady Ducayne rose from her chair, assisted by her crutch-stick, and Miss Torpinter escorted her to the door.

'And with regard to salary?' questioned the Person on the way.

'Salary, oh, the same as usual--and if the young woman wants a quarter's pay in advance you can write to me for a cheque,' Lady Ducayne answered, carelessly.

Miss Torpinter went all the way downstairs with her client, and waited to see her seated in the yellow chariot. When she came upstairs again she was slightly out of breath, and she had resumed that superior manner which Bella had found so crushing.

'You may think yourself uncommonly lucky, Miss Rolleston,' she said. 'I have dozens of young ladies on my books whom I might have recommended for this situation--but I remembered having told you to call this afternoon--and I thought I would give you a chance.

Old Lady Ducayne is one of the best people on my books. She gives her companion a hundred a year, and pays all travelling expenses. You will live in the lap of luxury.'

'A hundred a year! How too lovely! Shall I have to dress very grandly? Does Lady Ducayne keep much company?'

'At her age! No, she lives in seclusion--in her own apartments--her French maid, her footman, her medical attendant, her courier.'

'Why did those other companions leave her?' asked Bella..'Their health broke down!'

'Poor things, and so they had to leave?'

'Yes, they had to leave. I suppose you would like a quarter's salary in advance?'

'Oh, yes, please. I shall have things to buy.'

'Very well, I will write for Lady Ducayne's cheque, and I will send you the balance--after deducting my commission for the year.'

'To be sure, I had forgotten the commission.'

'You don't suppose I keep this office for pleasure.'

'Of course not,' murmured Bella, remembering the five shillings entrance fee; but nobody could expect a hundred a year and a winter in Italy for five shillings.

CHAPTER III

'From Miss Rolleston, at Cap Ferrino, to Mrs Rolleston, in Beresford Street, Walworth.

'How I wish you could see this place, dearest; the blue sky, the olive woods, the orange and lemon orchards between the cliffs and the sea--sheltering in the hollow of the great hills--and with summer waves dancing up to the narrow ridge of pebbles and weeds which is the Italian idea of a beach! Oh, how I wish you could see it all, mother dear, and bask in this sunshine, that makes it so difficult to believe the date at the head of this paper. November! The air is like an English June-the sun is so hot that I can't walk a few yards without an umbrella. And to think of you at Walworth while I am here! I could cry at the thought that perhaps you will never see this lovely coast, this wonderful sea, these summer flowers that bloom in winter. There is a hedge of pink geraniums under my window, mother--a thick, rank hedge, as if the flowers grew wild---and there are Dijon roses climbing over arches and palisades all along the terrace-a rose garden full of bloom in November! Just picture it all! You could never imagine the luxury of this hotel.

It is nearly new, and has been built and decorated regardless of expense. Our rooms are upholstered in pale blue satin, which shows up Lady Ducayne's parchment complexion; but as she sits all day in a corner of the balcony basking in the sun, except when she is in her carriage, and all the evening in her armchair close to the fire, and never sees anyone but her own people, her complexion matters very little.

'She has the handsomest suite of rooms in the hotel. My bedroom is inside hers, the sweetest room--all blue satin and white lace--white enamelled furniture, looking-glasses on every wall, till I know my pert little profile as I never knew it before. The room was really meant for Lady Ducayne's dressing-room, but she ordered one of the blue satin couches to be arranged as a bed for me-the prettiest little bed, which I can wheel near the window on sunny mornings, as it is on castors and easily moved about. I feel as if Lady Ducayne were a funny old grandmother, who had suddenly appeared in my life, very, very rich, and very, very kind.

'She is not at all exacting. I read aloud to her a good deal, and she dozes and nods while I read.

Sometimes I hear her moaning in her sleep--as if she had troublesome dreams. When she is tired of my reading she orders Francine, her maid, to read a French novel to her, and I hear her chuckle and groan now and then, as if she were more interested in those books than in Dickens or Scott. My French is not good enough to follow Francine, who reads very quickly. I have a great deal of liberty, for Lady Ducayne often tells me to run away and amuse myself;

I roam about the hills for hours. Everything is so lovely. I lose myself in olive woods, always climbing up and up towards the pine woods above--and above the pines there are the snow mountains that just show their white peaks above the dark hills. Oh, you poor dear, how can I ever make you understand what this place is like--you, whose poor, tired eyes have only the opposite side of Beresford Street? Sometimes I go no farther than the terrace in front of the hotel, which is a favourite lounging-place with everybody. The gardens lie below, and the tennis courts where I sometimes play with a very nice girl, the only person in the hotel with whom I have made friends. She is a year older than I, and has come to Cap Ferrino with her brother, a doctor--or a medical student, who is going to be a doctor. He passed his M.B. exam at Edinburgh just before they left home, Lotta told me. He came to Italy entirely on his sister's account. She had a troublesome chest attack last summer and was ordered to winter abroad. They are orphans, quite alone in the world, and so fond of each other. It is very nice for me to have such a friend as Lotta. She is so thoroughly respectable. I can't help using that word, for some of the girls in this hotel go on in a way that I know you would shudder at. Lotta was brought up by an aunt, deep down in the country, and knows hardly anything about life. Her brother won't allow her to read a novel, French or English, that he has not read and approved.

'"He treats me like a child," she told me, "but I don't mind, for it's nice to know somebody loves me, and cares about what I do, and even about my thoughts."'

'Perhaps this is what makes some girls so eager to marry--the want of someone strong and brave and honest and true to care for them and order them about. I want no one, mother darling, for I have you, and you are all the world to me. No husband could ever come between us two. If I ever were to marry he would have only the second place in my heart. But I don't suppose I ever shall marry, or even know what it is like to have an offer of marriage. No young man can afford to marry a penniless girl nowadays. Life is too expensive.'

'Mr Stafford, Lotta's brother, is very clever, and very kind. He thinks it is rather hard for me to have to live with such an old woman as Lady Ducayne, but then he does not know how poor we are-you and I--and what a wonderful life this seems to me in this lovely place. I feel a selfish wretch for enjoying all my luxuries, while you, who want them so much more than I, have none of them--hardly know what they are like--do you, dearest?--for my scamp of a father began to go to the dogs soon after you were married, and since then life has been all trouble and care and struggle for you.'

This letter was written when Bella had been less than a month at Cap Ferrino, before the novelty had worn off the landscape, and before the pleasure of luxurious surroundings had begun to cloy. She wrote to her mother every week, such long letters as girls who have lived in closest companionship with a mother alone can write; letters that are like a diary of heart and mind. She wrote gaily always; but when the new year began Mrs Rolleston thought she detected a note of melancholy under all those lively details about the place and the people.

'My poor girl is getting homesick,' she thought. 'Her heart is in Beresford Street.'

It might be that she missed her new friend and companion, Lotta Stafford, who had gone with her brother for a little tour to Genoa and Spezzia, and as far as Pisa. They were to return before February; but in the meantime Bella might naturally feel very solitary among all those strangers, whose manners and doings she described so well.

The mother's instinct had been true. Bella was not so happy as she had been in that first flush of wonder and delight which followed the change from Walworth to the Riviera. Somehow, she knew not how, lassitude had crept upon her. She no longer loved to climb the hills, no longer flourished her orange stick in sheer gladness of heart as her light feet skipped over the rough ground and the coarse grass on the mountain side. The odour of rosemary and thyme, the fresh breath of the sea, no longer filled her with rapture. She thought of Beresford Street and her mother's face with a sick longing. They were so far--so far away! And then she thought of Lady Ducayne, sitting by the heaped-up olive logs in the over-heated salon--thought of that wizened-nut--cracker profile, and those gleaming eyes, with an invincible horror.

Visitors at the hotel had told her that the air of Cap Ferrino was relaxing--better suited to age than to youth, to sickness than to health. No doubt it was so. She was not so well as she had been at Walworth; but she told herself that she was suffering only from the pain of separation from the dear companion of her girlhood, the mother who had been nurse, sister, friend, flatterer, all things in this world to her. She had shed many tears over that parting, had spent many a melancholy hour on the marble terrace with yearning eyes looking westward, and with her heart's desire a thousand miles away.

She was sitting in her favourite spot, an angle at the eastern end of the terrace, a quiet little nook sheltered by orange trees, when she heard a couple of Riviera habitués talking in the garden below. They were sitting on a bench against the terrace wall.

She had no idea of listening to their talk, till the sound of Lady Ducayne's name attracted her, and then she listened without any thought of wrong-doing. They were talking no secrets--just casually discussing an hotel acquaintance.

They were two elderly people whom Bella only knew by sight. An English clergyman who had wintered abroad for half his lifetime; a stout, comfortable, well-to-do spinster, whose chronic bronchitis obliged her to migrate annually.

'I have met her about Italy for the last ten years,' said the lady; 'but have never found out her real age.

'I put her down at a hundred--not a year less,' replied the parson. 'Her reminiscences all go back to the Regency. She was evidently then in her zenith; and I have heard her say things that showed she was in Parisian society when the First Empire was at its best--before Josephine was divorced.'

'She doesn't talk much now.'

'No; there's not much life left in her. She is wise in keeping herself secluded. I only wonder that wicked old quack, her Italian doctor, didn't finish her off years ago.'

'I should think it must be the other way, and that he keeps her alive.'

'My dear Miss Manders, do you think foreign quackery ever kept anybody alive?'

'Well, there she is--and she never goes anywhere without him. He certainly has an unpleasant countenance.'

'Unpleasant,' echoed the parson, 'I don't believe the foul fiend himself can beat him in ugliness. I pity that poor young woman who has to live between old Lady Ducayne and Dr Parravicini.'

'But the old lady is very good to her companions.'

'No doubt. She is very free with her cash; the servants call her good Lady Ducayne. She is a withered old female

Croesus, and knows she'll never be able to get through her money, and doesn't relish the idea of other people enjoying it when she's in her coffin. People who live to be as old as she is become slavishly attached to life. I daresay she's generous to those poor girls---but she can't make them happy. They die in her service.'

'Don't say they, Mr Carton; I know that one poor girl died at Mentone last spring.'

'Yes, and another poor girl died in Rome three years ago. I was there at the time. Good Lady Ducayne left her there in an English family. The girl had every comfort. The old woman was very liberal to her--but she died. I tell you, Miss Manders, it is not good for any young woman to live with two such horrors as Lady Ducayne and Parravicini.. They talked of other things--but Bella hardly heard them. She sat motionless, and a cold wind seemed to come down upon her from the mountains and to creep up to her from the sea, till she shivered as she sat there in the sunshine, in the shelter of the orange trees in the midst of all that beauty and brightness.

Yes, they were uncanny, certainly, the pair of them--she so like an aristocratic witch in her withered old age; he of no particular age, with a face that was more like a waxen mask than any human countenance Bella had ever seen. What did it matter? Old age is venerable, and worthy of all reverence; and Lady Ducayne had been very kind to her. Dr Parravicini was a harmless, inoffensive student, who seldom looked up from the book he was reading. He had his private sitting-room, where he made experiments in chemistry and natural science-perhaps in alchemy.

What could it matter to Bella? He had always been polite to her, in his far-off way. She could not be more happily placed than she was--in this palatial hotel, with this rich old lady.

No doubt she missed the young English girl who had been so friendly, and it might be that she missed the girl's brother, for Mr Stafford had talked to her a good deal--had interested himself in the books she was reading, and her manner of amusing herself when she was not on duty.

You must come to our little salon when you are "off," as the hospital nurses call it, and we can have some music. No doubt you play and sing?' upon which Bella had to own with a blush of shame that she had forgotten how to play the piano ages ago.

Mother and I used to sing duets sometimes between the lights, without accompaniment,' she said, and the tears came into her eyes as she thought of the humble room, the half-hour's respite from work, the sewing-machine standing where a piano ought to have been, and her mother's plaintive voice, so sweet, so true, so dear.

Sometimes she found herself wondering whether she would ever see that beloved mother again. Strange forebodings came into her mind. She was angry with herself for giving way to melancholy thoughts.

One day she questioned Lady Ducayne's French maid about those two companions who had died within three years.

'They were poor, feeble creatures,' Francine told her. 'They looked fresh and bright enough when they came to Miladi; but they ate too much and they were lazy. They died of luxury and idleness. Miladi was too kind to them. They had nothing to do; and so they took to fancying things; fancying the air didn't suit them, that they couldn't sleep.'

'I sleep well enough, but I have had a strange dream several times since I have been in Italy.'

'Ah, you had better not begin to think about dreams, or you will be like those other girls. They were dreamers--and they dreamt themselves into the cemetery.'

The dream troubled her a little, not because it was a ghastly or frightening dream, but on account of sensations which she had never felt before in sleep--a whirring of wheels that went round in her brain, a great noise like a whirlwind, but rhythmical like the ticking of a gigantic clock: and then in the midst of this uproar as of winds and waves she seemed to sink into a gulf of unconsciousness, out of sleep into far deeper sleep--total extinction. And then, after that blank interval, there had come the sound of voices, and then again the whirr of wheels, louder and louder--and again the blank-

-and then she knew no more till morning, when she awoke, feeling languid and oppressed.

She told Dr Parravicini of her dream one day, on the only occasion when she wanted his professional advice. She had suffered rather severely from the mosquitoes before Christmas---and had been almost frightened at finding a wound upon her arm which she could only attribute to the venomous sting of one of these torturers. Parravicini put on his glasses, and scrutinized the angry mark on the round, white arm, as Bella stood before him and Lady Ducayne with her sleeve rolled up above her elbow.

'Yes, that's rather more than a joke,' he said, 'he has caught you on the top of a vein. What a vampire! But there's no harm done, signorina, nothing that a little dressing of mine won't heal.

You must always show me any bite of this nature. It might be dangerous if neglected. These creatures feed on poison and disseminate it.'

'And to think that such tiny creatures can bite like this,' said Bella; 'my arm looks as if it had been cut by a knife.'

'If I were to show you a mosquito's sting under my microscope you wouldn't be surprised at that,' replied Parravicini.

Bella had to put up with the mosquito bites, even when they came on the top of a vein, and produced that ugly wound. The wound recurred now and then at longish intervals, and Bella found Dr Parravicini's dressing a speedy cure. If he were the quack his enemies called him, he had at least a light hand and a delicate touch in performing this small operation.

'Bella Rolleston to Mrs Rolleston--April 14th.

'Ever Dearest,--Behold the cheque for my second quarter's salary--five and twenty pounds.

There is no one to pinch off a whole tenner for a year's commission as there was last time, so it is all for you, mother, dear. I have plenty of pocket-money in hand from the cash I brought away with me, when you insisted on my keeping more than I wanted. It isn't possible to spend money here--except on occasional tips to servants, or sous to beggars and children--unless one had lots to spend, for everything one would like to buy--tortoise-shell, coral, lace-is so ridiculously dear that only a millionaire ought to look at it. Italy is a dream of beauty: but for shopping, give me Newington Causeway.

'You ask me so earnestly if I am quite well that I fear my letters must have been very dull lately. Yes, dear, I am well--but I am not quite so strong as I was when I used to trudge to the West-end to buy half a pound of tea--just for a constitutional walk--or to Dulwich to look at the pictures. Italy is relaxing; and I feel what the people here call "slack". But I fancy I can see your dear face looking worried as you read this. Indeed, and indeed, I am not ill. I am only a little tired of this lovely scene--as I suppose one might get tired of looking at one of Turner's pictures if it hung on a wall that was always opposite one. I think of you every hour in every day--think of you and our homely little room--our dear little shabby parlour, with the armchairs from the wreck of your old home, and Dick singing in his cage over the sewing-machine. Dear, shrill, maddening Dick, who, we flattered ourselves, was so passionately fond of us. Do tell me in your next that he is well.

'My friend Lotta and her brother never came back after all. They went from Pisa to Rome.

Happy mortals! And they are to be on the Italian lakes in May; which lake was not decided when Lotta last wrote to me. She has been a charming correspondent, and has confided all her little flirtations to me. We are all to go to Bellaggio next week--by Genoa and Milan. Isn't that lovely? Lady Ducayne travels by the easiest stages--except when she is bottled up in the train de luxe. We shall stop two days at Genoa and one at Milan. What a bore I shall be to you with my talk about Italy when I come home.

'Love and love-and ever more love from your adoring, Bella.'

CHAPTER IV

Herbert Stafford and his sister had often talked of the pretty English girl with her fresh complexion, which made such a pleasant touch of rosy colour among all those sallow faces at the Grand Hotel. The young doctor thought of her with a compassionate tenderness--her utter loneliness in that great hotel where there were so many people, her bondage to that old, old woman, where everybody else was free to think of nothing but enjoying life. It was a hard fate; and the poor child was evidently devoted to her mother, and felt the pain of separation-only two of them, and very poor, and all the world to each other,' he thought.

Lotta told him one morning that they were to meet again at Bellaggio. 'The old thing and her court are to be there before we are,' she said. 'I shall be charmed to have Bella again. She is so bright and gay--in spite of an occasional touch of homesickness. I never took to a girl on a short acquaintance as I did to her.'

'I like her best when she is homesick,' said Herbert; 'for then I am sure she has a heart.'

'What have you to do with hearts, except for dissection? Don't forget that Bella is an absolute pauper. She told me in confidence that her mother makes mantles for a West-end shop. You can hardly have a lower depth than that.'

'I shouldn't think any less of her if her mother made match-boxes.'

'Not in the abstract--of course not. Match-boxes are honest labour. But you couldn't marry a girl whose mother makes mantles.'

'We haven't come to the consideration of that question yet,' answered Herbert, who liked to provoke his sister.

In two years' hospital practice he had seen too much of the grim realities of life to retain any prejudices about rank. Cancer, phthisis, gangrene, leave a man with little respect for the outward differences which vary the husk of humanity. The kernel is always the same--fearfully and wonderfully made--a subject for pity and terror.

Mr Stafford and his sister arrived at Bellaggio in a fair May evening. The sun was going down as the steamer approached the pier; and all that glory of purple bloom which curtains every wall at this season of the year flushed and deepened in the glowing light. A group of ladies were standing on the pier watching the arrivals, and among them Herbert saw a pale face that startled him out of his wonted composure.

'There she is,' murmured Lotta, at his elbow, 'but how dreadfully changed. She looks a wreck.'

They were shaking hands with her a few minutes later, and a flush had lighted up her poor pinched face in the pleasure of meeting.

'I thought you might come this evening,' she said. 'We have been here a week.'

She did not add that she had been there every evening to watch the boat in, and a good many times during the day. The Grand Bretagne was close by, and it had been easy for her to creep to the pier when the boat bell rang. She felt a joy in meeting these people again; a sense of being with friends; a confidence which Lady Ducayne's goodness had never inspired in her.

'Oh, you poor darling, how awfully ill you must have been, exclaimed Lotta, as the two girls embraced.

Bella tried to answer, but her voice was choked with tears.

'What has been the matter, dear? That horrid influenza, I suppose?'

'No, no, I have not been ill--I have only felt a little weaker than I used to be. I don't think the air of Cap Ferrino quite agreed with me.'

'It must have disagreed with you abominably. I never saw such a change in anyone. Do let Herbert doctor you. He is fully qualified, you know. He prescribed for ever so many influenza patients at the Londres. They were glad to get advice from an English doctor in a friendly way.'

'I am sure he must be very clever!' faltered Bella, 'but there is really nothing the matter. I am not ill, and if I were ill, Lady Ducayne's physician--'

'That dreadful man with the yellow face? I would as soon one of the Borgias prescribed for me. I hope you haven't been taking any of his medicines.'

'No, dear, I have taken nothing. I have never complained of being ill.'

This was said while they were all three walking to the hotel. The Staffords' rooms had been secured in advance, pretty ground-floor rooms, opening into the garden. Lady Ducayne's statelier apartments were on the floor above.

'I believe these rooms are just under ours,' said Bella.

'Then it will be all the easier for you to run down to us,' replied Lotta, which was not really the case, as the grand staircase was in the centre of the hotel.

'Oh, I shall find it easy enough,' said Bella. 'I'm afraid you'll have too much of my society.

Lady Ducayne sleeps away half the day in this warm weather, so I have a good deal of idle time; and I get awfully moped thinking of mother and home.'

Her voice broke upon the last word. She could not have thought of that poor lodging which went by the name of home more tenderly had it been the most beautiful that art and wealth ever created. She moped and pined in this lovely garden, with the sunlit lake and the romantic hills spreading out their beauty before her. She was homesick and she had dreams: or, rather, an occasional recurrence of that one bad dream with all its strange sensations--it was more like a hallucination than dreaming--the whirring of wheels; the sinking into an abyss; the struggling back to consciousness. She had the dream shortly before she left Cap Ferrino, but not since she had come to Bellaggio, and she began to hope the air in this lake district suited her better, and that those strange sensations would never return.

Mr Stafford wrote a prescription and had it made up at the chemist's near the hotel. It was a powerful tonic, and after two bottles, and a row or two on the lake, and some rambling over the hills and in the meadows where the spring flowers made earth seem paradise, Bella's spirits and looks improved as if by magic.

'It is a wonderful tonic,' she said, but perhaps in her heart of hearts she knew that the doctor's kind voice and the friendly hand that helped her in and out of the boat, and the watchful care that went with her by land and lake, had something to do with her cure.

'I hope you don't forget that her mother makes mantles,' Lotta said, warningly.

'Or match-boxes: it is just the same thing, so far as I am concerned.'

'You mean that in no circumstances could you think of marrying her?'

'I mean that if ever I love a woman well enough to think of marrying her, riches or rank will count for nothing with me. But I fear--I fear your poor friend may not live to be any man's wife.'

'Do you think her so very ill?'

He sighed, and left the question unanswered.

One day, while they were gathering wild hyacinths in an upland meadow, Bella told Mr Stafford about her bad dream.

'It is curious only because it is hardly like a dream,' she said. 'I daresay you could find some common-sense reason for it. The position of my head on my pillow, or the atmosphere, or something.'

And then she described her sensations; how in the midst of sleep there came a sudden sense of suffocation; and then those whirring wheels, so loud, so terrible; and then a blank, and then a coming back to waking consciousness.

'Have you ever had chloroform given you--by a dentist, for instance?'

'Never--Dr Parravicini asked me that question one day.

'Lately?'

'No, long ago, when we were in the train de luxe.'

'Has Dr Parravicini prescribed for you since you began to feel weak and ill?'

'Oh, he has given me a tonic from time to time, but I hate medicine, and took very little of the stuff. And then I am not ill, only weaker than I used to be. I was ridiculously strong and well when I lived at Walworth, and used to take long walks every day. Mother made me take those tramps to Dulwich or Norwood, for fear I should suffer from too much sewing-machine; sometimes--but very seldom--she went with me. She was generally toiling at home while I was enjoying fresh air and exercise. And she was very careful about our food--that, however plain it was, it should be always nourishing and ample. I owe at to her care that I grew up such a great, strong creature.'

'You don't look great or strong now, you poor dear,' said Lotta.

'I'm afraid Italy doesn't agree with me.'

'Perhaps it is not Italy, but being cooped up with Lady Ducayne that has made you ill.'

'But I am never cooped up. Lady Ducayne is absurdly kind, and lets me roam about or sit in the balcony all day if I like. I have read more novels since I have been with her than in all the rest of my life.'

'Then she is very different from the average old lady, who is usually a slave-driver,' said Stafford. 'I wonder why she carries a companion about with her if she has so little need of society.'

'Oh, I am only part of her state. She is inordinately rich--and the salary she gives me doesn't count. Apropos of Dr Parravicini, I know he is a clever doctor, for he cures my horrid mosquito bites.'

'A little ammonia would do that, in the early stage of the mischief. But there are no mosquitoes to trouble you now.'

'Oh, yes, there are, I had a bite just before we left Cap Ferrino.

She pushed up her loose lawn sleeve, and exhibited a scar, which he scrutinized intently, with a surprised and puzzled look.

'This is no mosquito bite,' he said.

'Oh, yes it is--unless there are snakes or adders at Cap Ferrino.'

'It is not a bite at all. You are trifling with me. Miss Rolleston--you have allowed that wretched Italian quack to bleed you. They killed the greatest man in modern Europe that way, remember. How very foolish of you.'

'I was never bled in my life, Mr Stafford.'

'Nonsense! Let me look at your other arm. Are there any more mosquito bites?'

'Yes; Dr Parravicini says I have a bad skin for healing, and that the poison acts more virulently with me than with most people.'

Stafford examined both her arms in the broad sunlight, scars new and old.

'You have been very badly bitten, Miss Rolleston,' he said, 'and if ever I find the mosquito I shall make him smart. But, now tell me, my dear girl, on your word of honour, tell me as you would tell a friend who is sincerely anxious for your health and happiness--as you would tell your mother if she were here to question you--have you no knowledge of any cause for these scars except mosquito bites--no suspicion even?'

'No, indeed! No, upon my honour! I have never seen a mosquito biting my arm. One never does see the horrid little fiends. But I have heard them trumpeting under the curtains, and I know that I have often had one of the pestilent wretches buzzing about me.

Later in the day Bella and her friends were sitting at tea in the garden, while Lady Ducayne took her afternoon drive with her doctor.

'How long do you mean to stop with Lady Ducayne, Miss Rolleston?' Herbert Stafford asked, after a thoughtful silence, breaking suddenly upon the trivial talk of the two girls.

'As long as she will go on paying me twenty-five pounds a quarter.'

'Even if you feel your health breaking down in her service?'

'It is not the service that has injured my health. You can see that I have really nothing to do---to read aloud for an hour or so once or twice a week; to write a letter once in a way to a London tradesman. I shall never have such an easy time with anybody else. And nobody else would give me a hundred a year.'

'Then you mean to go on till you break down; to die at your post?'

'Like the other two companions? No! If ever I feel seriously ill--really ill--I shall put myself in a train and go back to Walworth without stopping.'

'What about the other two companions?'

'They both died. It was very unlucky for Lady Ducayne. That's why she engaged me; she chose me because I was ruddy and robust. She must feel rather disgusted at my having grown white and weak. By-the-bye, when I told her about the good your tonic had done me, she said she would like to see you and have a little talk with you about her own case.

'And I should like to see Lady Ducayne. When did she say this?'

'The day before yesterday.'

'Will you ask her if she will see me this evening?'

'With pleasure I wonder what you will think of her? She looks rather terrible to a stranger; but Dr Parravicini says she was once a famous beauty.'

It was nearly ten o'clock when Mr Stafford was summoned by message from Lady Ducayne, whose courier came to conduct him to her ladyship's salon. Bella was reading aloud when the visitor was admitted; and he noticed the languor in the low, sweet tones, the evident effort.

'Shut up the book,' said the querulous old voice. 'You are beginning to drawl like Miss Blandy.'

Stafford saw a small, bent figure crouching over the piled-up olive logs; a shrunken old figure in a gorgeous garment of black and crimson brocade, a skinny throat emerging from a mass of old Venetian lace, clasped with diamonds that flashed like fire-flies as the trembling old head turned towards him.

The eyes that looked at him out of the face were almost as bright as the diamonds--the only living feature in that narrow parchment mask. He had seen terrible faces in the hospital--faces on which disease had set dreadful marks--but he had never seen a face that impressed him so painfully as this withered countenance, with its indescribable horror of death outlived, a face that should have been hidden under a coffin-lid years and years ago.

The Italian physician was standing on the other side of the fireplace, smoking a cigarette, and looking down at the little old woman brooding over the hearth as if he were proud of her.

'Good evening, Mr Stafford; you can go to your room, Bella, and write your everlasting letter to your mother at Walworth,' said Lady Ducayne. 'I believe she writes a page about every wild flower she discovers in the woods and meadows. I don't know what else she can find to write about,' she added, as Bella quietly withdrew to the pretty little bedroom opening out of Lady Ducayne's spacious apartment. Here, as at Cap Ferrino, she slept in a room adjoining the old lady's.

'You are a medical man, I understand, Mr Stafford.'

'I am a qualified practitioner, but I have not begun to practise.'

'You have begun upon my companion, she tells me.'

'I have prescribed for her, certainly, and I am happy to find my prescription has done her good; but I look upon that improvement as temporary. Her case will require more drastic treatment.

'Never mind her case. There is nothing the matter with the girl--absolutely nothing--except girlish nonsense; too much liberty and not enough work.'

'I understand that two of your ladyship's previous companions died of the same disease,' said Stafford, looking first at Lady Ducayne, who gave her tremulous old head an impatient jerk, and then at Parravicini, whose yellow complexion had paled a little under Stafford's scrutiny.

'Don't bother me about my companions, sir,' said Lady Ducayne. 'I sent for you to consult you about myself--not about a parcel of anæmic girls. You are young, and medicine is a progressive science, the newspapers tell me. Where have you studied?'

'In Edinburgh--and in Paris.'

'Two good schools. And you know all the new-fangled theories, the modern discoveries--that remind one of the mediæval witchcraft, of Albertus Magnus, and George Ripley; you have studied hypnotism--electricity?'

'And the transfusion of blood,' said Stafford, very slowly, looking at Parravicini.

'Have you made any discovery that teaches you to prolong human life--any elixir--any mode of treatment? I want my life prolonged, young man. That man there has been my physician for thirty years. He does all he can to keep me alive--after his lights. He studies all the new theories of all the scientists--but he is old; he gets older every day--his brain-power is going--he is bigoted--prejudiced--can't receive new ideas--can't grapple with new systems. He will let me die if I am not on my guard against him.'

'You are of an unbelievable ingratitude, Ecclenza,' said Parravicini.

'Oh, you needn't complain. I have paid you thousands to keep me alive. Every year of my life has swollen your hoards; you know there is nothing to come to you when I am gone. My whole fortune is left to endow a home for indigent women of quality who have reached their ninetieth year. Come, Mr Stafford, I am a rich woman. Give me a few years more in the sunshine, a few years more above ground, and I will give you the price of a fashionable London practice--I will set you up at the West-end.'

'How old are you, Lady Ducayne?'

'I was born the day Louis XVI was guillotined.'

'Then I think you have had your share of the sunshine and the pleasures of the earth, and that you should spend your few remaining days in repenting your sins and trying to make atonement for the young lives that have been sacrificed to your love of life.'

'What do you mean by that, sir?'

'Oh, Lady Ducayne, need I put your wickedness and your physician's still greater wickedness in plain words? The poor girl who is now in your employment has been reduced from robust health to a condition of absolute danger by Dr Parravicini's experimental surgery; and I have no doubt those other two young women who broke down in your service were treated by him in the same manner. I could take upon myself to demonstrate--by most convincing evidence, to a jury of medical men--that Dr Parravicini has been bleeding Miss Rolleston, after putting her under chloroform, at intervals, ever since she has been in your service. The deterioration in the girl's health speaks for itself; the lancet marks upon the girl's arms are unmistakable; and her description of a series of sensations, which she calls a dream, points unmistakably to the administration of chloroform while she was sleeping. A practice so nefarious, so murderous, must, if exposed, result in a sentence only less severe than the punishment of murder.'

'I laugh,' said Parravicini, with an airy motion of his skinny fingers; 'I laugh at once at your theories and at your threats. I, Parravicini Leopold, have no fear that the law can question anything I have done.'

'Take the girl away, and let me hear no more of her,' cried Lady Ducayne, in the thin, old voice, which so poorly matched the energy and fire of the wicked old brain that guided its utterances. 'Let her go back to her mother--I want no more girls to die in my service. There are girls enough and to spare in the world, God knows.'

'If you ever engage another companion--or take another English girl into your service, Lady Ducayne, I will make all England ring with the story of your wickedness.'

'I want no more girls. I don't believe in his experiments. They have been full of danger for me as well as for the girl-- an air bubble, and I should be gone. I'll have no more of his dangerous quackery. I'll find some new man--a better man than you, sir, a discoverer like Pasteur, or Virchow, a genius- -to keep me alive. Take your girl away, young man. Marry her if you like.

I'll write her a cheque for a thousand pounds, and let her go and live on beef and beer, and get strong and plump again. I'll have no more such experiments. Do you hear, Parravicini?' she screamed, vindictively, the yellow, wrinkled face distorted with fury, the eyes glaring at him.

The Staffords carried Bella Rolleston off to Varese next day, she very loth to leave Lady Ducayne, whose liberal salary afforded such help for the dear mother. Herbert Stafford insisted, however, treating Bella as coolly as if he had been the family physician, and she had been given over wholly to his care.

'Do you suppose your mother would let you stop here to die?' he asked. 'If Mrs Rolleston knew how ill you are, she would come post haste to fetch you.'

'I shall never be well again till I get back to Walworth,' answered Bella, who was low-spirited and inclined to tears this morning, a reaction after her good spirits of yesterday.

'We'll try a week or two at Varese first,' said Stafford. 'When you can walk half-way up Monte Generoso without palpitation of the heart, you shall go back to Walworth.'

'Poor mother, how glad she will be to see me, and how sorry that I've lost such a good place.'

This conversation took place on the boat when they were leaving Bellaggio. Lotta had gone to her friend's room at seven o'clock that morning, long before Lady Ducayne's withered eyelids had opened to the daylight, before even Francine, the French maid, was astir, and had helped to pack a Gladstone bag with essentials, and hustled Bella downstairs and out of doors before she could make any strenuous resistance.

'It's all right.' Lotta assured her. 'Herbert had a good talk with Lady Ducayne last night and it was settled for you to leave this morning. She doesn't like invalids, you see.'

'No,' sighed Bella, 'she doesn't like invalids. It was very unlucky that I should break down, just like Miss Tomson and Miss Blandy.'

'At any rate, you are not dead, like them,' answered Lotta, 'and my brother says you are not going to die.'

It seemed rather a dreadful thing to be dismissed in that off-hand way, without a word of farewell from her employer.

'I wonder what Miss Torpinter will say when I go to her for another situation,' Bella speculated, ruefully, while she and her friends were breakfasting on board the steamer.

'Perhaps you may never want another situation,' said Stafford.

'You mean that I may never be well enough to be useful to anybody?'

'No, I don't mean anything of the kind.'

It was after dinner at Varese, when Bella had been induced to take a whole glass of Chianti, and quite sparkled after that unaccustomed stimulant, that Mr Stafford produced a letter from his pocket.

'I forgot to give you Lady Ducayne's letter of adieu,' he said.

'What, did she write to me? I am so glad--I hated to leave her in such a cool way; for after all she was very kind to me, and if I didn't like her it was only because she was too dreadfully old.'

She tore open the envelope. The letter was short and to the point:

'Goodbye, child. Go and marry your doctor. I enclose a farewell gift for your trousseau.---Adeline Ducayne.'

'A hundred pounds, a whole year's salary--no--why, it's for a--A cheque for a thousand!' cried Bella. 'What a generous old soul! She really is the dearest old thing.'

'She just missed being very dear to you, Bella,' said Stafford.

He had dropped into the use of her Christian name while they were on board the boat. It seemed natural now that she was to be in his charge till they all three went back to England.

'I shall take upon myself the privileges of an elder brother till we land at Dover,' he said; 'after that--well, it must be as you please.'

The question of their future relations must have been satisfactorily settled before they crossed the Channel, for Bella's next letter to her mother communicated three startling facts.

First, that the enclosed cheque for £1,000 was to be invested in debenture stock in Mrs Rolleston's name, and was to be her very own, income and principal, for the rest of her life.

Next, that Bella was going home to Walworth immediately.

And last, that she was going to be married to Mr Herbert Stafford in the following autumn.

'And I am sure you will adore him, mother, as much as I do,' wrote Bella. 'It is all good Lady Ducayne's doing. I never could have married if I had not secured that little nest-egg for you.

Herbert says we shall be able to add to it as the years go by, and that wherever we live there shall be always a room in our house for you. The word "mother-in-law" has no terrors for him.'